Alphabet
of Girls

Leland B. Jacobs

Alphabet of Girls

illustrated by Ib Ohlsson

· A Bill Martin Book ·

Henry Holt and Company

New York

Bill Martin Jr, Ph.D., has devoted his life to the education of young children. *Bill Martin Books* reflect his philosophy: that children's imaginations are opened up through the play of language, the imagery of illustration, and the permanent joy of reading books.

Henry Holt and Company, Inc.
Publishers since 1866
115 West 18th Street
New York, New York 10011
Henry Holt is a registered
trademark of Henry Holt and Company, Inc.
Text copyright © 1969 by Leland Jacobs
Illustrations copyright © 1994 by Ib Ohlsson
Published in Canada by Fitzhenry & Whiteside Ltd.,
195 Allstate Parkway, Markham, Ontario L3R 4T8.

Library of Congress Cataloging-in-Publication Data
Jacobs, Leland B. (Leland Blair).
Alphabet of girls / by Leland Jacobs; illustrated by
Ib Ohlsson.
"A Bill Martin book."
Summary: A rhyme for each letter of the alphabet tells
of the activities of girls whose names begin with that letter.
[1. Alphabet.   2. Stories in rhyme.]   I. Ohlsson, Ib,
ill.   II. Title.
PZ8.3.J138A1   1994   [E]—dc20   93-8328

ISBN 0-8050-3018-2

First Revised Edition—1994
Printed in the United States of America
on acid-free paper. ∞
1   3   5   7   9   10   8   6   4   2

For Beatrice
—L. B. J.

For Helle
—I. O.

A

Arabella, Araminta,
Audrey, too, and Ann
Played at keeping house,
As all girls can.

Arabella fed the baby;
Araminta made the tea;
Ann put out the cups and saucers;
Audrey came as company.

Araminta washed the dishes;
Ann arranged them on the shelf;
Arabella bathed the baby;
Audrey sat and rocked herself.

Little Betsy Buttoncup
Counted up to seven,
Turned about, and bobbed about,
And counted to eleven.

Little Betsy Buttoncup,
She could count a-plenty:
Six, eleven, eight, eleven,
Ten, eleven, twenty!

Carol has a scuffed-up knee,
And Carla has a cold.
Charlotte has the chicken pox—
That's what I've been told.

Carla can't come out to play,
Nor Charlotte—obviously.
Carol isn't any fun.
She frets about her knee.

Carrie's sewing for her dolls,
And Cora's gone away.
I guess I've found the recipe
To make a lonely day.

D

Doris skips,
  Dolores prances,
Delia scurries,
  Della dances,
Daphne walks
  With queenly grace,
Dolly always
  Wins the race,
Darcy marches,
  Donna ambles,
Dorothy lopes,
  And Dora scrambles.
Almost every
  Girl you meet
Has some special way
  With feet.

In the early evening,
Evelyn and Esther
Sat and watched the sun go down,
Lost in cloudy hallways.
When the evening star came out,
Evelyn and Esther
Closed their eyes and wished a wish
That they'd be friends for always.

F

Faye believes
    In fairy folk.
Florence thinks
    That's quite a joke.

(Fleuretta, dainty
    And demure,
Is in between.
    She isn't sure.)

Florence asks
    If Faye has seen
Fairies dancing
    On the green.

Has she caught
    One in a net?
Faye replies
    She hasn't yet.

(Fleuretta notes
    You'd have to wait
To see them dance
    Till very late.)

Florence goes
    On arguing
There is no
    Magic fairy ring.

But Faye's belief
    Is hard to sway.
She's certain
    Fairies live today.

(Fleuretta, who
    Is always kind,
Simply won't
    Make up her mind.)

There's something wrong
With Greta today.
She sits and reads
In a listless way.

And something happened
To Gwendolyn.
She's practicing her violin.
Yesterday, you may recall,
She wouldn't try
A tune at all.

And Genevieve
Just mopes about.
She's in her room
And won't come out.
She says we all
Should keep away—
She's much too tired
To want to play.

The breeze is warm.
The day is bright.
Do you suppose
They had a .....?
The way they act,
With each one hid,
I'll bet they did,
I'll bet they did!

H

Hilda's birthday comes, we know,
Wrapped in January's snow.

Harriet's birthday comes on wings
Of March's windy wanderings.

Hope can celebrate her day
With sun-etched greenery, in May.

For Heather's birthday, all the birds,
In August, sing their summer words.

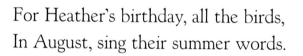

Hazel's natal day will hold
October's scarlet and its gold.

Holly's day, in mid-December,
Is the easiest to remember.

I

Ida's eyes are fawn brown.
Her bangs are chestnut. And,
When she goes out into the sun,
Her nose gets nicely tanned.

Ivy's eyes are sea-green.
Her pigtails gleam like gold.
And in the summer sun, her nose
Is spread with freckles bold.

Ila's eyes are sky-blue.
Each reddish ringlet turns.
And when the sun is hot, her nose
Just burns and burns and burns.

J

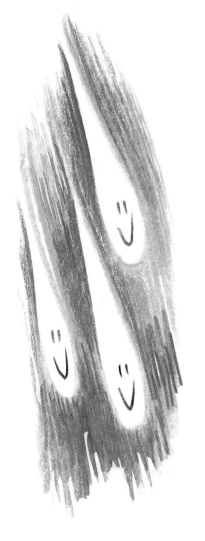

Jennifer, Josephine,
    Jill, and Jane
All went out
    For a walk in the rain.

"Rubbers are rain feet,"
    Josephine said.
And Jennifer nodded
    Her hooded head.

"Umbrellas are mushrooms
    That grow in the rain,"
Said Jill and laughed—
    And so did Jane.

The girls all laughed
    At the jokes they knew
As they walked in the rain—
    And the rain laughed too.

K

When Kate and Karen
Have their battles,
Katherine tattles.

When Kay and Katherine
Have a spat,
Kate tells that.

When Katherine and Kate
Their tempers lose,
Kay spreads the news.

But Karen gets
The greatest glory.
She turns a friendly fight
Into a full-length story,
And makes it gory.

L

Lou's afraid of caterpillars
With their furry humps.
Lillian's afraid of frogs,
Or anything that jumps.

Lena fears the lightning's flash
The thunder's crash and roar.
Luella dreads the dashing waves
That pound upon the shore.

Laura frets about the wind
That moans and rants at night.
Lily thinks a spider
Is a very scary sight.

Though I pretend I have no fears,
It's really all a sham.
And I'm afraid they'll all find out
How much afraid I am.

I whistled to Mae
With the golden hair.
She looked about with
    A puzzled stare.

I whistled to Mollie,
Whose red hair glistens.
She skipped down the street.
    She never listens.

I whistled to Meg—
Her hair is black.
She tossed her head, and
    She whistled back.

Nellie tried
To knit a sweater.
Knitting wasn't
Nellie's lot.
Other people
Knit much better.
Nellie's knitting
Was a KNOT.

Ora, Ora,
Why do you giggle?
I have a tooth
With a looselike wiggle.

Ola, Ola,
Why do you grin?
I have a new tooth
Coming in.

Olive, Olive,
Why do you shout?
I have a tooth
that has just come out!

When Polly's with Patricia,
A sundae's what they eat,
And when she's with Penelope,
A soda is the treat.

With Paulette, she eats sherbet,
Though when she is alone,
She orders what she'd always choose—
A two-dip chocolate cone.

Queenie's strong and Queenie's tall.
You should see her bat a ball,
Ride a bike, or climb a wall.
(Queenie's not her name at all.)

Queenie's nimble, Queenie's quick.
You should see her throw a stick,
Watch her saw a board that's thick,
See her do her tumbling trick.

Queenie's not afraid, like me,
Of snakes or climbing up a tree.
(I think that's why the boys agree,
Queenie's what her name should be.)

R

Roseanna,
      Rosella,
            Rosedith, and Rose—
How odd! Not a one of them,
Goodness knows,
Resembles that flower.
I've thought long and hard,
And they're not like that posy
In any regard.

Roseanna's a violet—delicate, shy.
Rosella's a tumbleweed, scampering by.
Rosedith's a buttercup, shiny as gold,
And Rose is a snowdrop, fond of the cold.

Rosedith,
      Roseanna,
            Rosella, and Rose—
Not one of them thinks of herself,
I suppose,
As being that flower
Their names would propose.
My name is Rosetta,
And everyone knows
I may be a daisy,
But never a rose!

S

Hello, Sarah.
    This is Sue.
I can come
    And play with you.

You get Sheila,
    I'll get Sadie.
We'll each dress up
    And be a lady.

We'll wear our hats
    And jewelry.
We'll chat and sew
    And all have tea.

You say you'd rather
    Make mud pie?
I'll come some
    Other day. Good-bye!

When Tina tells stories,
    We all gather round.
Everyone's quiet—
    There isn't a sound.
We all like the stories
    That Tina relates
Of princes and towers
    And creaky old gates.

She tells of a poor girl
    Who went to a ball,
But it's nothing like
    Cinderella at all.
And wee folks, says Tina,
    Even when big,
Are so small they can hide
    By the tiniest twig.

She tells of enchantments,
    Of witchery too,
Of princesses married,
    And wishes come true.
When Tina tells stories,
    Time turns to a stone,
And all of the magic
    Is really our own.

Needles and pins,
Needles and pins,
Una and Ura are
Look-alike twins.

Think-alike, dress-alike
Twins are they,
Always together,
Every day.
Whether they laugh,
Or whether they stitch,
It's troublesome telling
Which is which.
Speak-alike, eat-alike
Girls, they play
The very same games
In the very same way.
At school, or out
On the avenue,
With Una and Ura,
Who is who?

Needles and pins,
Needles and pins,
Una and Ura are
Say-alike, play-alike,
Talk-alike, walk-alike,
Like-alike twins.

Vera Virginia
   Vaguely goes
Hither and thither,
   Led by her nose.

And if we ask her
   Where she went,
She looks at us
   In astonishment.

If we inquire,
   "Where *did* you go?"
She answers vaguely,
   "To and fro."

Or ask her where
   She went to play,
She says, "Nearby
   And far away."

Or voice the question,
   "You've been *where*?"
She tells us vaguely,
   "Here and there."

So "up and down"
Or "high and low"
Or "roundabout"
Is all we know

Of places
Vera Virginia's been—
Except, once out,
She now is in.

When window-shopping,
    Wanda stares
At what a grown-up
    Lady wears.

And Wilhelmina
    Feasts her eyes
On doughnuts, cookies,
    Cakes, and pies.

Wilda always
    Says she needs
To see what's new
    In rings and beads.

Winona's different
    From the rest.
She likes the hardware
    Windows best.

X

She wishes her name was different,
Like Caroline or Marie.
But they named her for Great-grandma,
Whose name turned out to be:
        Xenobia.

She wishes her name was pretty,
Like Leslie, Annette, or Lou.
But there it is, Great-grandma's name—
And hers, her whole life through:
        Xenobia.

If you were to ask her parents,
They'd say it's such a shame
How she always makes an awful fuss
About the lovely name:
        Xenobia.

She is my friend—my special friend—
The one I most prefer.
She wishes her name was different,
And I agree with her—
        Xenobia.

Yolanda, Yolanda,
Yolanda is her name.
She dances like a butterfly,
She dances like a flame.
She dances like a summer breeze,
A ripple at the shore.
Yolanda! Please, Yolanda,
Dance for us some more.

Zepha plays the zither,
And Zelda's always with her—
Zelda's always with her,
  Playing on a comb.

Their playing is so zealous
That no one needs to tell us—
We know what just befell us—
  The girls are home!

Zepha's zither strumming
And Zelda's comb a-humming
Warn us what is coming,
  Through the live-long day.

There is no use in saying
Their din is not dismaying.
We wish they'd take their playing
  Far, far away!